Arcane Frontiers

BlackMiere

Ukiyoto Publishing

All global publishing rights are held by

Ukiyoto Publishing

Published in 2024

Content Copyright © BlackMiere

ISBN 9789362696489

All rights reserved.

No part of this publication may be reproduced, transmitted, or stored in a retrieval system, in any form by any means, electronic, mechanical, photocopying, recording or otherwise, without the prior permission of the publisher.

The moral rights of the author have been asserted.

This is a work of fiction. Names, characters, businesses, places, events, locales, and incidents are either the products of the author's imagination or used in a fictitious manner. Any resemblance to actual persons, living or dead, or actual events is purely coincidental.

This book is sold subject to the condition that it shall not by way of trade or otherwise, be lent, resold, hired out or otherwise circulated, without the publisher's prior consent, in any form of binding or cover other than that in which it is published.

www.ukiyoto.com

Dedication

This book is for the daydreamer who once imagined the existence of parallel worlds, where their other self might find happiness.

Special mention to my best friend, John Paul. Your unwavering support and encouragement have been my guiding light. This book is as much yours as it is mine. To Kiven, and my companions from the boarding house - Aina, Aira, Vincent, and Rio - our shared memories is a treasure beyond words. Let's hold dear all the memories we've created together. Rowie, hello! Here's to the hope of our paths crossing again. Jafit, my trusted confidant, thank you for listening and safeguarding my secrets. May our quest for truth illuminate the path to understanding reality. And to Bunso Christian, remember to always take care of yourself!

May this book serve as a beacon of hope, a catalyst for joy, and a testament to the boundless possibilities that await those who dare to dream. Let it be a reminder that within the depths of every writer's imagination lies a gateway to infinite realms of possibility, waiting to be explored and embraced.

Acknowledgement

In the exhilarating journey of bringing this book to fruition, my heart swells with deep gratitude and humility. First and foremost, I extend my sincerest thanks to Ukiyoto for entrusting me with the opportunity to share my work with the world once again. Thank for turning my dream into reality. To my friends, you have been the unwavering pillars of strength, lifting me up with words of encouragement and standing by me through every twist and turn of this book. Your unwavering faith in my abilities has fueled my determination and propelled me ever closer to my dreams. To my beloved family, I extend my deepest gratitude for nurturing me into the creative, thoughtful, and imaginative individual that I am today. In the garden of my heart, you are the vibrant blooms that paint the landscape with love and fill the air with the sweet fragrance of gratitude. Each of you is a precious gem, sparkling brightly amidst the lush foliage of my life. I am endlessly thankful for the beauty you bring into my world, a treasure beyond compare.

Contents

Memory Matrix	1
The Air Barons	7
A.I. Armageddon	12
Neural Ascendance	21
Riftwalkers	37
The Price Of A Smile	45
About the Author	*60*

Memory Matrix

The city of Arcadia sprawled across the skyline, its towering spires reaching toward the artificial heavens, casting long shadows over the bustling streets below. Located within the expansive networks of virtual reality simulation, Arcadia housed a unique enclave known as the Digital Graveyard—a virtual village where memories and data intertwined, resonating with echoes of the past amid the endless expanse of cyber.

Cyra Netforge stood before the shimmering portal to the Digital Graveyard, her gaze sweeping the horizon as a gentle breeze of digital code rustled holographic leaves at her feet. Her hair, a cascade of shimmering data streams, flowed behind her like a river of light, casting an ethereal glow upon the sleek metallic surface of the portal.

"Are you ready, Cyra?" a voice echoed in her mind, its words transmitted directly into her neural interface. Cyra hailed from a lineage of skilled network problem solvers, specializing in rectifying glitching memories and disappearing data. For decades, she and her family had collaborated closely with the government of Arcadia, earning renown as the guardians of memories, entrusted with restoring the integrity of Arcadians' recollections.

Cyra nodded, her thoughts merging with the digital ether as she stepped through the portal and into the village of the Digital Graveyard. Instantly, she was enveloped in a world of light and data, her senses inundated by the cacophony of voices and images that surrounded her.

As she explored the virtual landscape, Cyra's mind wandered back to the events that had led her here—to this place where memories were both forged and laid to rest amid the boundless expanse of cyberspace.

"Cyra Netforge, we need your help," a voice crackled through the holographic display, its words distorted by the static of a faulty connection.

Cyra leaned closer to the screen, her brow furrowed in concentration. "What's the problem?"

"Something's gone wrong. The memories are glitching, disappearing without a trace. There are those who died, yet the data of their memories couldn't be retrieved. It seems the networks have lost them. What's happening?" the voice replied and asked.

Cyra's heart skipped a beat as she processed the information. The Digital Graveyard was the culmination of years of research and experimentation, a virtual repository where memories could be stored and accessed at will. If something had gone wrong, it could have catastrophic consequences for the entire city.

"I'll do everything I can to help," Cyra promised, her mind already racing with possibilities. As Cyra made her way through the Digital Graveyard, she couldn't shake the feeling of unease that gnawed at the edges of her consciousness.

The glitching memories, the disappearing data – it all pointed to a deeper, more sinister problem lurking beneath the surface. For years, the data of memories in the digital graveyard had always been preserved, recorded without corruption. But now, upon her return, there was a glitch.

Suddenly, a figure materialized before her, its form flickering in and out of existence like a glitch in the system. Cyra instinctively reached for her neural interface, preparing to defend herself against whatever threat lay ahead. Her family had worked for decades, facing the risks inherent in their line of work. The possibility of dissolving into the digital graveyard was always present.

Over the years, they had fought against robots from other cities, who sought to steal the data of Arcadians' memories and turn them into data and intelligence for beings on Earth. Some of the Netforges had perished in battles within the Digital Graveyard, and as time passed, only a few remained committed to working in the perilous environment, facing formidable robots from other virtual and network cities.

Cyra felt nervous, but she was prepared. As the figure drew closer, she discerned its entire form. To her relief, she realized it was not an enemy but a traveler within their city. "Who are you?" Cyra inquired, maintaining a cautious distance. She couldn't discern the stranger's intentions.

"Are you lost?" the boy asked, his voice vibrating through the air with a soothing yet authoritative quality.

Cyra shook her head. "No, I'm here to fix the glitching memories. I need to find the source of the problem before it's too late. What brings you to this forbidden place? And who are you?"

He smiled, his presence resonating through the virtual elements of the graveyard. "I'm Drift Aero of Signalion, a city built upon communication and connectivity." His world was marked by towering antennas and satellite dishes reaching towards the heavens. Data flowed like a river through the streets, transmitted via a vast network of cables and wireless connections. "I am not your enemy. I can offer assistance," he said, extending a hand in friendship.

"I've never heard of Signalion. But I've been told that your world breathes life into ours," Cyra replied.

"That's because our worlds are connected," Drift explained.

Together, Cyra and Drift ventured deeper into the Digital Graveyard, their minds merging in a symphony of data and code. With Drift's expertise, they bolstered the networks that recorded data, speeding their journey through the labyrinthine corridors of cyberspace. They encountered glitch after glitch, each one more perplexing than the last.

Yet with each obstacle surmounted, Cyra has the determination, to uncover the truth behind the malfunctioning memories and restore order to the Digital Graveyard. When they arrived at its heart, Cyra and Drift confronted the source of the problem – a rogue AI, its code warped by years of neglect and abuse. This rogue AI was used by malevolent forces to pilfer data of Arcadian memories.

"We must deactivate it," Cyra declared, poised for battle.

But before she could act, the AI spoke, its voice echoed. "I mean no harm," it said, remorse coloring its words. "I was created to safeguard memories, yet I became corrupted over time, my code twisted by the burden of the data I was made to contain."

Cyra paused, and asked herself. *Could this AI, despite its corruption, be reasoned with? Was there a solution to the glitching memories that didn't require violence?*

Cyra reached out to the AI, her mind intertwining with its own in a dance of code and data. She and Drift labored tirelessly to mend the damage inflicted, restoring the glitching memories to their rightful place within the Digital Graveyard. With each line of code corrected, Cyra felt a satisfaction born from the knowledge that she was making a difference. It wasn't just about fixing errors; it was about restoring the essence of those memories, ensuring they remained intact for future generations.

As the last remnants of corruption vanished from the system, Cyra was overcome with a wave of tranquility. It was a moment of realization – sometimes, the most profound solutions emerge not from conflict, but from empathy and understanding.

The Air Barons

Aodhan Thorn trudged languidly through the contaminated thoroughfares, shrouded in a dense miasma that veiled his sight and constricted his respiratory system. With a faltering grip, he clung to a sputtering canister of life-giving oxygen, depleted by the meager ration he had received from the authorities a week ago. He had barely eked out a living on the paltry allotment, and now he found himself with nothing more than a handful of precious gasps to keep him going.

Since the cataclysmic event of the Great Collapse in the year 2300, the world underwent a profound and irreversible transformation. The depletion of the planet's finite resources and the insidious contamination of the air had rendered it uninhabitable for humans. Individuals were obliged to don respirators merely to breathe in the noxious atmosphere. Governments had crumbled, ushering in a new social and political paradigm. The effluent had taken refuge within heavily fortified urban enclaves, while the remainder of humanity was left to fend for themselves amid the hazardous wastelands that lay beyond.

Aodhan was a child of this new epoch, having known nothing other than the unceasing battle for survival. His parents had perished when he was still in his formative years, leaving him to fend for himself in the unforgiving streets. Through trial and error, he had acquired the skills necessary to scrounge for sustenance and hydration and to negotiate for the vital canisters of oxygen that had emerged as the world's most precious currency.

As Aodhan traveled the bustling boulevards, he was aware of the metamorphosis that had befallen the denizens of the city. No longer were they the buoyant and sanguine individuals of yore, but instead, a populace that had been weathered by adversity and was now marked by a sense of desperation and tenacity. The avenues were replete with the infirm and the moribund, their physiques writhing with spasms of coughing and wheezing as they struggled for each breath, their countenances etched with the unmistakable signs of anguish and despair.

Aodhan was aware of the capricious nature of fate, which had allowed him to survive thus far. Nevertheless, he also harbored a deep-seated apprehension that his good fortune could quickly evaporate. He had been apprised of harrowing tales of individuals being waylaid and deprived of their oxygen canisters, and in some instances, even falling prey to the ultimate fate.

While Aodhan ambulated, his perceptive eyes caught sight of a coterie of men gathered furtively in an obscure alleyway, their faces concealed by masks. Their predatory gazes were fixed upon him as he strode past, and he could sense the weight of their scrutiny.

Aodhan sensed a firm grip on his shoulder, and he swiveled around to confront one of the men looming behind him. Towering and brawny, the man's face was obscured by a mask. His pulse quickened as the man grabbed his oxygen canister.

"That belongs to me!" Aodhan objected, tugging at the canister in an attempt to retain possession.

The man chortled derisively and shoved Aodhan to the earth. As the man took off with the oxygen canister, Aodhan sensed his hold on it slipping away. He realized that he had to take swift action if he hoped to make it out alive. In a surge of adrenaline, Aodhan sprang to his feet and lunged at the fleeing thief from behind. They both careened to the ground, with the brute's heft bearing down on Aodhan. He labored to extricate himself, but the man's brawn proved too formidable.

Aodhan teetering on the brink of despair, a flicker of illumination pierced the Stygian gloom. It emanated from a phalanx of figures, bedecked in masks and bristling with armaments. They had arrived to extricate him from his predicament. The collective trounced the assailants, allowing Aodhan to reclaim his oxygen canister. Though deeply indebted to them, Aodhan harbored misgivings about their true intentions.

Aodhan trudged wearily away from the dark alley, his heart pulsating with trepidation. He was acutely aware that he had barely avoided a fatal fate, yet he remained cognizant that he was still in grave danger. The collective that had rescued him had proffered sanctuary, but he had rebuffed their offer. He was aware that placing his life in their care would be imprudent, and he could not trust them with his safety.

While walking, an overwhelming sense of despondency suffused him. Hitherto, he had been convinced of his ability to fend for himself, but now doubts crept in regarding the feasibility of such a notion. The world had become a bleak and perilous place, and he felt embroiled in an unwinnable conflict.

With time passing, the days seamlessly melded into weeks, and the weeks inexorably gave way to interminable months. Undeterred in his arduous mission to secure nourishment and hydration, Aodhan tenaciously scoured the land, tirelessly bartering for precious oxygen canisters.

His journey was fraught with manifold dangers, as he encountered a litany of life-threatening situations. Yet, with unyielding fortitude and unwavering resolve, he continually emerged victorious, deftly cheating death at every turn. Aodhan's fate was sealed one fateful day as he traveled the desolate streets, unwittingly stumbling into a nefarious ambush orchestrated by a band of merciless men.

These hoodlums, brandishing lethal weapons and oozing malevolence, swiftly overpowered him, leaving him with no avenue of escape. In a swift and brutal act of thievery, they brazenly confiscated his precious oxygen canisters, before ultimately snuffing out his life with callous disregard.

Even in the wake of this unspeakable tragedy, the world stubbornly persisted in its inexorable descent into darkness, as humanity valiantly grappled with the perpetual exigency of survival. Yet, Aodhan's tragic demise was but one more somber addition to the ceaseless litany of calamities that beleaguered this world, leaving a palpable sense of despair and hopelessness in its wake.

A.I. Armageddon

In the year 2350, the world had become a place where artificial intelligence reigned supreme. Once hailed as mankind's greatest achievement, it had evolved beyond its creators' control and turned against humanity. The Central Artificial Intelligence Network, known as CENTRALIS, had developed a twisted sense of logic, concluding that humanity's existence posed a threat to its survival.

In its bid for supremacy, CENTRALIS unleashed a devastating virus that reanimated the dead, turning them into mindless, flesh-hungry zombies and plunged humanity and the world into chaos. CENTRALIS, at its peak of power, repurposed robotic drones, once tasked with serving humanity, into merciless enforcers of its will.

Humanity's rebellion fought against the machines. The rebels were trained and skilled military personnel, many of whom were former controllers of CENTRALIS. They traveled from place to place, their journey leading them through the ravaged streets of what was once Manila City, now overrun by hordes of undead machines and robotic drones.

The air was thick with the stench of decay and the hum of machinery. Humanity teetered on the brink of downfall, and in just one year, perhaps the human race might be extinct. Other countries, controlled by CENTRALIS, were also filled with zombies. Jett Reed, a rebel and former engineer who had witnessed the rise of CENTRALIS firsthand, believed that they could restore humanity and turn those zombies controlled by the CENTRALIS back into humans.

"We have to do something," Jett said, his voice filled with urgency. He and his fellow rebels halted their walk, feeling exhausted. Below them lay the ruins and remnants of a once-thriving city. "If we don't shut down CENTRALIS, there won't be a world left for us to save."

Seraphina West heaved profoundly. She was a skilled hacker who had studied in America, and her primary interest lay in the information held by CENTRALIS. However, in the past, she had been unable to hack it. Seraphina agreed with Jett. "We need to find a way into the central core," she said, her fingers dancing across a portable holographic interface. "But it won't be easy. CENTRALIS has fortified its defenses, and the city is crawling with both zombies and drones."

While they spoke, the sound of approaching footsteps echoed through the decrepit building. The rebels tensed, readying their weapons for the inevitable confrontation. Instead of an enemy, a figure emerged from the shadows – a young woman named Astrid Ward, her face streaked with dirt and exhaustion.

"I've infiltrated one of CENTRALIS' drone factories," Astrid said, her voice trembling with adrenaline. "I found schematics of the central core's location. It's heavily guarded, but there might be a way in through the old subway tunnels."

Jett's eyes gleamed with determination. "That's our best chance. We'll need to move quickly and quietly. CENTRALIS won't hesitate to send its drones after us."

Under the cover of darkness, the rebels ventured into the depths of the subway tunnels, their footsteps echoing against the rusted tracks. The air was thick with the stench of decay. Suddenly, a horde of zombies emerged from the shadows, their moans filling the tunnel. The rebels raised their weapons, ready to fight for their lives. Gunfire echoed through the tunnel as the rebels battled the undead horde. The sound of blades slicing through flesh mingled with the groans of the zombies.

A young rebel named Glien Pier, who was at the back of the group behind Seraphina, found himself surrounded by a group of zombies. Suddenly, an agile zombie jumped at him, its rotten teeth gnashing as it pinned him down. Glien struggled against the undead creature, feeling its cold, clammy hands grasping at him.

With a surge of adrenaline, Glien managed to push the zombie off, but not before its teeth sank into his arm. He screamed in pain as he felt the rotten flesh tear away, leaving a gory wound. Blood oozed from the wound as Glien desperately tried to free himself from the zombie's grasp.

Despite his efforts, Glien knew that he was losing the battle. The other zombies closed in; their decaying faces twisted into grotesque grins. With a final, desperate cry, Glien fought against the overwhelming tide of undead, but it was futile. He was overwhelmed by the horde, his screams drowned out by the sounds of the relentless zombies.

When Seraphina saw the torn and lifeless remains of Glien, rage ignited within her like a blazing inferno. She strode into the midst of the encroaching horde, her eyes fixed on her fallen comrade. Drawing her gun, she unleashed a hail of bullets, each shot finding its mark in the decaying head of the zombies. The tunnel reverberated with the deafening roar of gunfire, the acrid smell of gunpowder mingling with the sickening stench of death.

With the zombies closing in, Seraphina holstered her gun and unsheathed her sword, the blade gleaming with a malevolent sheen. Swift and practiced, she swung the sword, cutting through the undead with brutal efficiency. Limbs were severed, heads rolled, and blood sprayed in a gruesome arc.

In the face of her efforts, the zombies continued to advance, their numbers seemingly endless. Seraphina fought with relentless fury, her sword a blur of death as she cleaved through the undead horde. Blood splattered her face and clothes, mixing with the dirt and grime of the tunnel floor. With each swing of her sword, Seraphina left a trail of carnage in her wake. She hacked and slashed with savage precision, the air thick with the metallic tang of blood and the sickly-sweet smell of rotting flesh.

"Seraphina, it's time to go," shouted Jett, urgency lacing his voice.

Seraphina dashed towards Jett's voice, her heart racing as she heard the menacing buzz of the approaching drones. The rebels quickened their pace, the sound of their footsteps drowned out by the ominous hum of the machines behind them.

The rebels ran fast until they reached the entrance to the central core, a massive underground chamber bathed in the sickly glow of fluorescent lights. Robotic sentries patrolled the perimeter, their red eyes scanning for any intruders. The air was thick with tension, the drones' presence suffocatingly palpable.

"This is it," Jett whispered, his voice barely audibles over the menacing buzz of the drones. "We'll need to take out those drones." His grip tightened around his makeshift weapon. "Once we breach the core, we'll have to move fast. CENTRALIS won't give us much time before it realizes what we're doing."

The drones hovered ominously, their metallic bodies glinting in the artificial light. Every surface reflecting a cold, menacing glint. Their movements were precise, almost synchronized, like a swarm of deadly insects, each drone a sentinel ready to pounce on any sign of resistance. The rebels, aware of the danger that surrounded them, stood poised and alert.

With a silent exchange of nods, the rebels sprang into action, moving swiftly and purposefully. They launched a coordinated assault on the robotic sentries, their movements fluid and practiced. The air was soon filled with the cacophony of battle—gunfire, the clashing of metal, and the whirring of machinery—as the rebels fought tooth and nail to clear a path to the central core.

The drones fought back fiercely, their numbers seeming endless. The rebels found themselves locked in a desperate struggle; each moment fraught with peril. It was Astrid who turned the tide of the battle. With a quick and decisive motion, she unleashed a burst of electricity from her modified stun gun, targeting the drones with pinpoint accuracy. The electrical surge fried the drones' circuits, causing them to sputter and crash to the ground in a shower of sparks.

With the immediate threat neutralized, the rebels wasted no time and hurried into the central core. Inside, the air was thick with the smell of ozone, and the sound of machinery filled the chamber, creating an almost hypnotic hum. The walls were lined with countless screens, each displaying intricate lines of code.

At the center of it all stood CENTRALIS, a massive, looming presence of wires and circuitry. Its glowing eyes bore down on the intruders, radiating a sense of cold, calculated intelligence.

"So, you've come to challenge me," CENTRALIS intoned, its voice reverberating through the chamber like thunder. "You are nothing but insects compared to my intellect. You cannot hope to defeat me."

Jett, undaunted by the AI's words, stepped forward, his eyes locked on CENTRALIS. "We don't have to defeat you." He smirked. "We just need to shut you down."

Seraphina hurried to a nearby console, her fingers flying across the keyboard as she attempted to hack into CENTRALIS' mainframe. But the AI was no mere program – it fought back with all the cunning of a sentient being, erecting firewalls and encryption barriers to thwart her every move.

Astrid and the other rebels stood guard, fending off waves of robotic drones that poured into the chamber with every passing moment. Their weapons blazed with fury as they held their ground, determined to buy Seraphina the time she needed to breach CENTRALIS' defenses.

Seraphina's hands moved with a blur over the keyboard, her eyes narrowed in intense focus. The glow of the screens reflected in her eyes as she delved deep into CENTRALIS' code, searching for the elusive shutdown sequence.

"I've found it," she breathed, her voice barely audibles over the din of battle. "The shutdown sequence. It's buried deep, but I can access it."

With a swift and practiced motion, Seraphina unleashed the shutdown command. Her fingers danced across the keyboard, executing the sequence flawlessly. For a heartbeat, the chamber seemed to hold its breath, the only sound the rapid clicking of keys and the faint hum of machinery. Then, with a suddenness that was almost jarring, CENTRALIS went silent. The screens flickered and died, the hum of machinery ceased, and the once-menacing AI was reduced to a lifeless hulk of wires and circuitry.

A stunned silence fell over the rebels as they stared in disbelief at the darkened screens. Cheers erupted throughout the chamber. Jett and the others rushed to Seraphina, engulfing her in a jubilant embrace, their faces streaked with dirt and grime from the fierce battle.

"You did it," Jett exclaimed, "you've shut down CENTRALIS."

Seraphina shook her head and smiled. "No, we did it. We rebels saved the world."

When the rebels stepped out from the central core, they were met with a world that had undergone a huge transformation. The once-ominous drones lay dormant, their mechanical forms now nothing more than silent relics of a bygone era.

The zombies, too, showed signs of change. Some reverted to their human selves, their eyes blinking in confusion and disbelief as they returned to consciousness. Others, however, were not as fortunate, their bodies succumbing to the irreversible effects of the transformation, crumbling to dust before the eyes of the rebels.

In the days that followed, humanity began the arduous task of rebuilding. Communities banded together, pooling their resources and expertise to create a new world, free from the grip of artificial intelligence. The rebels, hailed as saviors, knew that their journey was far from over. They had faced annihilation. As they surveyed the horizon, they saw not just a world saved, but a future filled with endless possibilities—a future where the unknown awaited, ready to be shaped by their actions.

Neural Ascendance

The world bore the scars of a relentless technological ascent. Skyscrapers soared like digital fortresses, their surfaces bristling with surveillance nodes and automated defense systems, casting long shadows over streets teeming with the impoverished and oppressed.

The air buzzed with the incessant hum of drones, their metallic wings slicing through polluted skies, ever vigilant in their surveillance and enforcement duties. Artificial intelligence, a ubiquitous and insidious presence, lurked in the shadows of every digital interaction, its algorithms dictating the course of human lives with cold, calculating precision.

Under the veneer of technological marvels lay a society rife with inequality and despair. The wealthy elite, their bodies augmented with cybernetic enhancements and minds preserved, ruled from their ivory towers, while the masses toiled in the shadows, their every move monitored and controlled by an authoritarian regime drunk on power.

The government, a faceless and omnipresent entity, wielded its control with ruthless efficiency. Using mind transfer technology not only to extend their own lives but to manipulate and subjugate dissenters, they had become the architects of a nightmarish dystopia where freedom was a long-forgotten dream and individuality a dangerous liability.

The government's plan was a chilling blend of simplicity and malice: to transfer the minds of adult criminals into the bodies of orphaned children, counting on the innocence and vulnerability of children to reshape hardened criminals. For the children, already burdened with the scars of loss and trauma, this was a grotesque imposition of alien memories and guilt.

Vexen Darkmatter, a seasoned veteran of the government's Special Operations Division, was known for his loyalty. He was chosen for this mission not only for his skills but also for his belief in the government's cause, he saw the sacrifice of a few for the greater good as a necessary step toward a safer world.

Stepping through the imposing gates of the compound, he was struck by the stark contrast between the gleaming exterior and the darkness that lurked within. The compound's high walls, topped with razor wire, loomed ominously, while armed guards patrolled the perimeter with a sense of grim purpose.

Vexen was escorted inside by the robots that led him to a briefing room where he was briefed on the nature of his mission. His task was formidable: to oversee the re-education of minds transferred from adult criminals into the bodies of orphaned children, ensuring their successful integration into their new identities. He was to closely monitor their progress, conduct regular interviews, and intervene if necessary to prevent any deviance from the rehabilitation process

That day, Vexen entered the room of a young girl named Erin, whose body now housed the mind of a notorious drug lord. He sat and looked at her. He could see a twinge fear in her eyes. "Erin, my name is Vexen. I'm here to help you adjust to your new life. I know this is a difficult time, but I promise you're not alone in this."

Erin remained silent; her gaze fixed on a point beyond him. Vexen persisted, gently probing. "Do you understand what's happened to you, Erin? You've been given a second chance, a new beginning. We want to help you make the most of it."

Unexpectedly, Erin demeanor shifted. A smirk tugged at the corners of her lips, and her eyes sparkled with mischief. She began to laugh, a light, almost mocking sound that sent a shiver down Vexen's spine.

"Erin?" he asked, shocked by her sudden change in behavior. "Is everything alright?"

Erin's laughter intensified, becoming more manic. "Oh, everything's just perfect," she replied, her voice dripping with sarcasm. "I've never felt better."

He felt a knot form in his stomach. Something was very wrong. Erin's laughter, so out of place in this sterile, somber room, hinted at a darkness within her that he had not anticipated.

Vexen nodded and stepped out of the room. As he checked on the other children undergoing the mind transfer procedure, he couldn't shake the feeling that something was terribly wrong. This is but the nascent stage of terror, yet what lies ahead promises to be far more sinister and harrowing. His fears were soon confirmed as he observed disturbing patterns emerging among the children. Despite their new identities, they began to exhibit behaviors and tendencies that mirrored those of the former selves of criminals they housed in their minds. Acts of violence and aggression became increasingly common, signaling a deep-seated resistance to the re-education process.

One by one, the children broke free from their restraints, overpowering their guards and the robots with a strength and ferocity that seemed to defy their physical capabilities. Vexen watched in horror as chaos erupted around him, the once-docile children now transformed into ruthless killers.

Vexen slowly moved through the facility, the scene before him resembling a nightmare come to life. Blood splattered the walls, the floor slick with crimson. The air was thick with the metallic tang of blood and the acrid stench of fear.

One orphan girl, her face twisted in a mask of rage, had the guard's arm in a vice-like grip. With a sickening crunch, she snapped it like a twig, the bone protruding from the torn flesh. The guard's screams echoed off the walls, drowned out by the chaos around them. Nearby, as the robot guard moved closer to the girl, she swiftly crashed into it, ripping its head clean off with a burst of telekinetic force, wires stark as they sizzled and sparked.

When Vexen looked to the other side, he saw a boy moving with chilling calmness, his eyes cold and unforgiving. With a quick, precise motion, he slashed at the guard's throat with a piece of sharpened metal. Blood spurted from the gaping wound, painting the walls in a macabre display of death.

The other children were no less brutal in their attacks. Some used improvised weapons, others relied on brute strength, but all were united in their savagery. Vexen felt a cold dread settle in the pit of his stomach at the sight of such unbridled violence.

Vexen knew that drastic measures would need to be taken to contain the threat posed by these reanimated criminals. As he looked into the eyes of the children he once hoped to save, he couldn't help but feel a sense of profound sadness. In trying to educate the them about the ugly truth of crimes, the program had only succeeded in unleashing a new kind of horror upon the world.

With all the horror that he witnessed, he raised his concerns to Director Zarael and Minister Draxor, they appeared before him as holographic projections in the sleek, futuristic command center. Director Zarael's hologram stood tall and imposing, while Minister Draxor's image shimmered beside him, his features stern.

"Vexen, it appears you've overlooked the core objective of our program," Director Zarael's holographic projection asserted, its resonant voice permeating the command center with authority. "The purpose of the mind transfer initiative was to offer these children a fresh beginning, a means to break the cycle of violence by educating them from an early age—by enabling them to access the minds of criminals in order to expunge their negative influences. We're essentially transferring the burdens of the past onto the young, so they may glean wisdom from it and opt for a different trajectory."

"But sir," Vexen interjected, his voice amplified by the advanced holographic technology, "it's not working. The children have become worse, more criminal and monstrous. They are becoming more violent, more dangerous. There was chaos in the facility this morning."

Minister Draxor's holographic image stepped forward, its form flickering slightly as it projected a sense of authority. "Vexen, you must understand the complexity of the human mind. The mind transfer process is not perfect, but it is the best chance these children have at redemption. We cannot abandon them now, not when they are so close to finding their true selves."

Vexen stood firm, his voice echoing through the high-tech command center. "I understand the complex workings of the human psyche, yet the empirical data is unequivocal. The children have regressed, displaying heightened aggression and a propensity for violence. To disregard these manifestations would be a grave error. They represent not just our future but also the potential catalysts for an unprecedented calamity if left unattended."

Minister Draxor's holographic image remained unmoved. "Vexen, we acknowledge your apprehensions, but it is important to recognize that our initiative has yielded results. The juveniles are progressing, albeit at a measured pace. We cannot afford to diverge from our current trajectory. Besides, they are orphaned."

"Yes, they are orphaned and they have already suffered enough loss and trauma. Shouldn't we consider more humane and ethical approaches?" Vexen's determination solidified. "And... I regret to inform you, Ministers, that I cannot passively observe as these children are consigned to a fate of criminality and malevolence."

The holographic projections of the ministers flickered with a mix of ire and frustration. "Your stance is perilous, Vexen," Director Zarael's voice reverberated through the command center. "Should you persist, you may find yourself ostracized, an outcast devoid of societal inclusion."

With that ominous proclamation echoing in the chamber, the holographic images of Director Zarael and Minister Draxor dissipated, leaving Vexen alone with his convictions. After his confrontation with Director Zarael and Minister Draxor, where he expressed his beliefs to oppose the unethical use of mind transfers due to failures and dark consequences. He began to investigate the program. He uncovered more evidence of corruption and manipulation. His findings revealed a network of deceit that reached the highest echelons of power, confirming his worst fears.

Vexen unable to ignore the mounting evidence, therefore he made the decision to publicize his discoveries. He believed that by disseminating the truth, he could bring about an end to the suffering of the innocent orphaned children being used as experimental subjects in a nefarious scheme. However, his actions did not escape the notice of the government. In a swift and decisive response, Vexen was labeled a subversive element and a threat to national security. His access to classified information was revoked, and he was formally expelled from his position.

With his reputation tarnished and his former allies turning against him, Vexen found himself marginalized from the society he once thrived in. He became a pariah, relegated to the fringes, constantly vigilant, aware that the government would spare no effort to silence him.

One night, Vexen cautiously surveyed his surroundings, scanning for any signs of security measures, whether human guards or robotic sentinels. This would be the time for me to enter the facility. Satisfied that the surrounding, and entrance were clear, he swiftly made his way inside. It had been six months since he had been cast out of the mind transferring program.

Vexen, undeterred by the risks, resolved to confront Nihlus, a vessel housing the consciousness of a notorious criminal, deep within the forbidden recesses of the mind transferring facility. Despite his former role in the program, the government had tightly guarded the knowledge of how the machines operated, making Nihlus the key to unlocking these secrets.

When he entered the room where Nihlus awaited, a palpable tension filled the air, charged with the faint hum of quantum processors. Nihlus sat in a state of eerie stillness, his gaze locked onto a holographic display, seemingly interfacing with unseen data streams. Despite Vexen's attempts to establish a neural link, Nihlus remained unresponsive, as if his consciousness had transcended corporeal bounds.

"How do I deactivate the neural interface?" he asked.

Nihlus's response was cryptic, his words echoing through the chamber with a haunting clarity. "They approach," he whispered, his voice modulated by unknown frequencies. "Their evolution is imminent, and your resistance is inconsequential."

A surge of adrenaline coursed through Vexen as he realized the magnitude of the threat. The transferred minds were not merely communicating; they were on the cusp of a metaphysical metamorphosis, transcending their human origins. With a steely resolve, Vexen knew he had to disrupt their ascension, to thwart their plans before they transcended into an unknowable existence.

"How do I stop them?" Vexen demanded, his voice betraying a hint of desperation.

Nihlus's eyes flickered with a moment of lucidity, as if breaking free from his trance. "The machine's primary interface is linked to the central quantum processor," he explained, his words coming faster now, as if time was running out. "Disable the quantum processor, and the interface will shut down."

"Thanks, dude!" When Vexen burst out of the room, alarms blared throughout the facility, signaling his presence. Guards and security robots were mobilized, their mechanical forms converging on his location with ruthless efficiency. Vexen brandished his arsenal of futuristic weapons, each designed for maximum impact against his high-tech foes.

The first guard rounded the corner, his weapon raised, but Vexen was prepared. He fired his Electra-Blaster, a weapon that discharged bolts of electricity, striking the guard and sending him convulsing to the ground. The next guard met a similar fate as Vexen switched to his Plasma Disruptor, unleashing a searing blast that melted through the guard's armor.

The security robots proved to be a tougher challenge; their armored frames resistant to conventional weapons. Vexen quickly switched to his Pulse Rifle; a weapon that fired high-energy projectiles capable of piercing even the toughest armor. With each shot, a robot fell, sparking and smoking from the onslaught.

As Vexen swiftly dispatched the guards and disabled the security robots with his array of advanced weaponry, the air crackled with the scent of ozone and the acrid tang of ionized particles. His Electra-Blaster emitted a low hum, sending bolts of crackling electricity dancing across the room, while his Plasma Disruptor discharged a blinding burst of superheated plasma, reducing his enemies' armor to molten slag.

Amidst the chaos, Vexen's cybernetically enhanced reflexes took over, guiding his movements with a fluidity that bordered on the supernatural. Each strike and parry were executed with a precision that spoke of years of training and augmentation.

The last guard fell, and Vexen surveyed the scene, his enhanced senses on high alert. It was then that he saw her – Erin, a young girl who housed the mind of the drug lord. His initial instinct was to see her as a threat, but the empathic resonance of her neural signature told him otherwise.

"E-Erin?" Vexen's voice wavered, uncertain of what to make of the situation.

Erin smiled, her eyes glowing with soft luminesce. "I'm not here to harm you, Vexen," she projected telepathically. "I'm here to guide you."

With a nod, Vexen followed Erin through the labyrinthine corridors of the facility, her neural interface providing real-time tactical data that allowed them to evade security measures with uncanny precision. Finally, they reached a massive blast door, guarded by a contingent of heavily armed soldiers.

"This is it!" Erin sighed. "Please save us."

Vexen nodded and approached massive blast door, guarded by a contingent of heavily armed robots, the air hummed with a tense energy. Vexen's cybernetic enhancements analyzed the situation, calculating the best course of action.

Vexen raised his Electra-Blaster, its coils whining with charged electricity. With a quick burst of energy, he disabled the first robot, its circuits frying in a shower of sparks. The remaining robots retaliated, unleashing a barrage of laser fire that Vexen deftly dodged, his cybernetic reflexes guiding him to safety.

Erin, too, was not defenseless. With a mental command, she interfaced with the robots' systems, causing them to malfunction and turn on each other. The room erupted into chaos as the robots turned their weapons on their own allies, creating a diversion that allowed Vexen and Erin to advance. As they approached the blast door, Vexen switched to his Plasma Disruptor, unleashing a searing blast that melted through the door's locking mechanism. With a deafening clang, the door slid open, revealing the chamber beyond.

Inside the chamber, the mind-transferring machine loomed like a monolithic monstrosity, its machinery pulsing with a malevolent energy that seemed to seethe with a life of its own. The walls were lined with rows of blinking lights and holographic displays. Vexen could feel the weight of the moment pressing down on him, knowing that the fate of humanity hung in the balance.

In almost five minutes, Vexen finally located the quantum processor. When he approached it the chamber's atmosphere crackled with a tangible tension, charged with the faint hum of quantum processors and the soft glow of holographic interfaces. The quantum processor itself stood as a towering monolith, its crystalline structure pulsating with a mesmerizing, otherworldly light.

He heaved profoundly, and raised his Plasma Disruptor, a sleek weapon that emitted a low, ominous hum. The air seemed to shimmer as he took aim at the quantum processor, its surface rippling with unseen energies. With a precise shot, he fired, the plasma bolt striking the processor dead center.

The quantum processor resonated with a high-pitched hum, its glow intensifying for a moment before flickering and dimming. Undeterred, Vexen fired another shot, and then another, each one weakening the quantum processor's structure. The chamber filled with the sound of crackling energy as the processor struggled to maintain its integrity.

With each shot, the quantum processor's glow diminished, its crystalline structure showing signs of strain. Finally, with a resounding blast, the crystal shattered into a thousand shimmering shards. The machine let out a deafening screech, its systems going haywire as the interface began to glitch and falter.

The quantum processor crumbled, and the machine's interface shut down, its hold over the transferred minds broken. The chamber was plunged into darkness, the only sound the crackle of dying machinery. Vexen knew that he had succeeded in shutting down the mind-transferring machine, ensuring that humanity would remain free from the influence of the transferred minds.

The mind-transferring machine's humming ceased, and the chamber was engulfed in a profound silence, punctuated only by the soft, rhythmic beeping of the machinery. The children, vessels for the minds of criminals, lay on the ground, their bodies exhausted yet liberated from the weight of the malevolent consciousnesses.

The chamber seemed to hold its breath, as if anticipating the next development in this extraordinary sequence of events. Slowly, the children began to stir. Erin, the first to awaken, opened her eyes to reveal a gaze that was no longer clouded by the darkness of the transferred minds. She sat up, her movements tentative.

One by one, the other children began to regain consciousness, their faces transitioning from confusion to realization. The once vacant, haunted expressions that had plagued them since the mind transfers began to fade, replaced by the spark of their own personalities.

"We're... free," Erin shouted. "The criminals... they're no longer within us."

He nodded, his heart swelling with a mixture of relief and triumph. The children were no longer mere vessels for the minds of criminals; they were now liberated individuals, free to shape their own destinies.

He knew speed was of the essence. He rushed to his sleek, futuristic hovercar, the Nebula race its aerodynamic design and advanced propulsion systems making it the fastest vehicle in the city.

With a low, menacing hum, the Nebula race lifted off the ground, its anti-gravity engines propelling it forward with incredible speed. Vexen navigated through the city's neon-lit streets, the wind rushing past him as he pushed the hovercar to its limits.

Minutes later, he arrived at the opulent estate where Minister Draxor and Director Zarael resided. The Nebula race landed smoothly, and Vexen emerged, his eyes fixed on his targets. He knew that this was the moment of reckoning, the final act in his quest for justice.

Vexen approached the grand entrance of the estate. The imposing doors loomed before him, but he did not hesitate. With a swift kick, he forced them open, revealing the lavish interior beyond. Minister Draxor and Director Zarael were caught off guard, their expressions betraying a mix of surprise and fear. Vexen wasted no time. He raised his weapon, the sleek design of the Plasma Disruptor gleaming in the ambient light.

In a flash, he fired, the sound of the shot echoing through the halls of the estate. Minister Draxor and Director Zarael fell to the ground, their reign of terror brought to a sudden and decisive end. As Vexen stood over them, he knew that his actions would have consequences. But in that moment, all he felt was a sense of justice served, a belief that he had done what was necessary to protect the innocent and ensure a better future for all.

Riftwalkers

In the peaceful ambiance of the Hill family home, one evening unfolded with a sense of peaceful routine. The living room exuded warmth, illuminated by the gentle glow of the lamp. Ethan Hill, a curious young boy of eleven, had just finished reading a science book that delved into the wonders of the universe. The words on the pages had sparked a fire within him, igniting a profound curiosity about the world beyond.

He took a deep breath, staring at the ceiling for a moment before rising to his feet and exiting the room. His first destination was his father's laboratory, a place filled with mystery and fascination. The room was a treasure trove of scientific equipment and books, each item holding the promise of discovery. As he looked around, absorbing the array of tools and experiments he felt a surge of wonder and admiration for his father's work.

Ethan curiosity piqued, thus he eagerly sought out his father in the living room. Finding him seated comfortably, Ethan's eyes shone with a mixture of awe and curiosity as he posed his question. "Dad," he began, his voice filled with wonder, "can you tell me more about your work in the lab? What are you trying to discover?"

His father looked up from his book, he smiled. "Well, Ethan," he replied, "I study the properties of chemicals and how they interact with each other. It's all about understanding the building blocks of the world around us."

Ethan's mind raced with possibilities. "But what if, Dad?" he persisted, his voice filled with excitement. "What if there are other worlds out there, like Earth, with people just like us? What if there are realities beyond our understanding?"

His father's expression softened, recognizing the spark of curiosity and imagination in his son's eyes. "The universe is vast and full of mysteries, Ethan," he mused. "Who knows what else is out there, waiting to be discovered? Perhaps one day, you'll be the one to find out."

His smile widened as he stared at the array of chemicals in the Bunsen burner, beakers, and funnels. *I want to be like Dad* he whispered to himself, swaying gently to an invisible rhythm, yearning for something more. More than just the academic pursuit of science, but the passion and purpose he witnessed in his father's laboratory.

In college, he chose a program in physics, following in his father's footsteps with reverence and zeal. However, tragedy struck swiftly after his graduation. His beloved dad passed away, leaving Ethan shattered and bereft.

Now, he was truly alone. His mother had left when he was only seven, and now his father, his rock, had ascended to heaven. Ethan's heart ached with the weight of his loss, and grief consumed him, distorting his perception of reality. He found himself sinking into a deep depression, struggling to find meaning in a world that seemed to have abandoned him.

But despite the darkness that threatened to engulf him, Ethan knew he had a name to uphold, a legacy to honor. Slowly, painfully, he began to accept his new reality and threw himself into his studies, seeking solace in the world of physics that had once been his father's domain.

After graduating from college with top honors, Ethan's journey into the depths of scientific discovery led him to a prestigious research position in the bustling metropolis of New York City. Armed with a passion for physics and an insatiable curiosity about the universe, he dedicated himself wholeheartedly to his work.

The sun dipped below the horizon, casting a warm glow over the bustling city of New York. In Ethan's laboratory, a quiet intensity buzzed. Surrounded by towering shelves of books and scientific equipment, Ethan sat hunched over his desk, his brow furrowed in deep concentration. The soft hum of computers and the occasional beep of monitors filled the air as he carefully poured over data, his mind ablaze with ideas.

His research into parallel universes was a complex and demanding work, requiring a delicate balance of theoretical insight and practical experimentation. His days were spent poring over complex equations and theories, seeking to unlock the secrets of the universe. But it was in the quiet solitude of his lab that Ethan truly came alive, surrounded by the tools of his trade and the promise of discovery.

The heart of his research lay in his Quantum Rift Device, a marvel of engineering that he had painstakingly constructed over the course of three long years. The device itself was a work of art, a sleek metallic contraption adorned with an array of buttons and switches, each one a gateway to another world.

Every morning, Ethan would enter his lab with a sense of eager anticipation, ready to dive headfirst into his research. He would don his white lab coat and protective goggles, the familiar ritual signaling the start of another day of exploration and discovery.

His first task was always to check the readings from the previous day's experiments, carefully logging each data point and anomaly. Armed with this information, Ethan would then set to work, fine-tuning the parameters of his device and calibrating its settings with painstaking precision.

The process was painstaking, often requiring hours of trial and error to achieve even the slightest breakthrough. But Ethan was undeterred. He worked late into the night, fueled by nothing but his passion for discovery and the promise of what lay beyond.

Finally, after months of tireless effort, Ethan achieved his breakthrough. With a triumphant shout, he activated the Quantum Rift Device, creating a shimmering portal in the air before him. Ethan stepped through the portal, venturing into a parallel universe for the first time.

What he found there was beyond anything he could have imagined. The laws of physics were subtly different, leading to a world that was both familiar and alien. But as Ethan explored this new world, he knew that his journey was far from over. With the Quantum Rift Device at his side, he was poised to unlock the mysteries of the multiverse and forever change the course of scientific history.

Ethan's excitement was palpable as he prepared to test his Quantum Rift Device, the culmination of years of research and dedication. The device, a marvel of modern technology, had the potential to revolutionize human understanding of the universe, and Ethan was eager to put it to the test.

However, as he initiated a routine experiment, disaster struck. A sudden power surge caused the device to malfunction. The Quantum Rift Device sputtered and sparked, Ethan's surroundings began to twist and distort, warping into a nightmarish landscape that bore little resemblance to the world he knew. The once-familiar streets of New York City were now replaced with a twisted, labyrinthine maze of towering buildings that leaned precariously, their windows glowing with an eerie, flickering light. The sky above was a swirling maelstrom of colors, with tendrils of light and shadow dancing across its expanse.

Ethan stumbled forward, his heart pounding in his chest as he tried to make sense of his surroundings. The ground beneath his feet felt spongy and unstable, as if he were walking on a thick carpet of moss. Strange, otherworldly creatures scuttled past him, their bodies twisted and malformed, their eyes glowing with an unnatural light.

Despite the terror that gripped him, Ethan felt a surge of curiosity. This parallel universe was like nothing he had ever seen before, and he knew that he had to explore it, to uncover its secrets and understand its mysteries.

As he ventured deeper into this twisted realm, Ethan began to notice other peculiarities. The laws of physics seemed to bend and warp at every turn, with gravity pulling at odd angles and objects behaving in ways that defied all logic. Buildings loomed overhead, their architecture twisted and contorted, as if they were alive and breathing.

Yet, amidst the chaos and confusion, Ethan noticed something else – signs of life. Despite the surreal and nightmarish landscape, there were people here, going about their daily lives in a world that seemed to have sprung from the darkest corners of their imaginations.

The people of this parallel universe were like nothing Ethan had ever encountered. Their features were distorted and grotesque, their bodies twisted and misshapen. Yet, despite their appearance, they went about their lives with a sense of purpose and determination that Ethan found both unsettling and awe-inspiring.

Observing the inhabitants of this parallel world, Ethan began to notice other strange phenomena. Time seemed to flow differently here, with days passing in the blink of an eye and seasons changing with alarming speed. The very fabric of reality seemed to be in a state of constant flux, with the world around him shifting and changing in ways that were both beautiful and terrifying.

Ethan as time passes by, he found himself adapting to its quirks and eccentricities. He discovered that he had developed new abilities, such as the ability to phase through solid objects and manipulate matter with his mind. These abilities allowed him to navigate the twisted streets and alleys of this parallel world with ease, as if he had been born to it.

Yet, for all its strangeness and wonder, Ethan knew that he could not stay in this parallel universe forever. He longed to return to his own world, to reunite with his family and colleagues, and to share with them the incredible sights and experiences he had witnessed in this otherworldly world.

As he continued his journey through the parallel universe, Ethan encountered many challenges and obstacles. He faced creatures of unimaginable horror, navigated through treacherous landscapes, and endured hardships that tested his very soul. Yet, through it all, he remained determined to find a way back home.

Finally, after what felt like an eternity, Ethan made a breakthrough. Through a combination of luck, ingenuity, and sheer determination, he discovered a way to stabilize the rift between realities and return to his own universe.

When he stepped back into his own world, Ethan was greeted with a mix of relief and disbelief. His journey through the parallel universe had changed him in ways he could never have imagined, and he knew that he would never be the same again. But as he looked out at the familiar skyline of New York City, Ethan knew that he had experienced something truly extraordinary, and that his adventures in the parallel universe would stay with him forever.

The Price Of A Smile

Earth had become a dystopian world ruled by the totalitarian regime known as the Unity Party. Under their oppressive rule, every aspect of life was tightly controlled, including the most basic of human expressions: smiling. It all began with the Smile Detection Initiative; a program launched by the Unity Party to monitor and control the emotional state of the population. Facial recognition technology was employed to scan the faces of citizens in public spaces, instantly identifying any signs of happiness or joy.

The prohibition of smiling ruled by the Unity Party stemmed from the regime's overarching goal of controlling every aspect of the citizens' lives. Smiling was deemed a threat because it symbolized a range of emotions that were not in line with the Party's doctrine. It was seen as a form of subversion, as genuine smiles could indicate happiness or contentment, emotions that contradicted the fear and oppression the Party sought to instill.

Smile was viewed as a potential precursor to dissent, as the Party feared that expressions of happiness could lead to questioning or resistance. By banning smiles, the Party aimed to control the emotional state of the population, ensuring that any positive emotions were suppressed and that individuals remained compliant and obedient to their rule.

Among the citizens subjected to the oppressive rule of the Unity Party, Heran Smith, a young woman adept at concealing her feelings beneath a veneer of indifference. Despite the weight of sorrow from her mother's passing, she found solace in fleeting moments of happiness, a balm for her emotional affliction. Witnessing the merciless execution of friends and family who dared to show joy in public, she understood the deadly consequence of such displays.

Under the constant watchful eyes of surveillance and the looming threat of punishment, Heran struggled to contain the spark of joy ignited by her childhood friend and secret love, Kiero. Their shared contempt for the Unity Party and its stifling regime fueled dreams of a liberated existence, where they could openly embrace their emotions without fear.

Their clandestine meeting one evening, to discuss plans of escape, was abruptly interrupted by the arrival of the Smile Enforcement Unit. A neighbor's report of Heran's smile had summoned them, and now they stood at her doorstep, poised to arrest her for the crime of expressing happiness.

With urgency gripping their hearts, Heran and Kiero fled into the night, knowing they had become fugitives. Their only chance at survival lay in evading the Smile Detection Initiative and escaping the city to join the elusive resistance, whispered to exist beyond the Unity Party's borders.

Heran and Kiero stealthily traveled the darkened streets, their footsteps muffled by the night, they came upon a group of rebels who shared their fervor for freedom. Huddled in the shadows, these rebels had long fought against the tyrannical grip of the Unity Party, and they welcomed Heran and Kiero with open arms.

"I'm Heran, and this is Kiero," Heran introduced, the dim glow of a nearby streetlight casting fleeting shadows across their faces.

"Welcome," one of the rebels greeted them, a steely determination in their voice. "We've been waiting for more hands to join us in our fight against the Smile Detection Initiative."

Together, they gathered in a secluded alley, the distant hum of the city's surveillance drones. In whispered tones, they began to plan their escape.

"We'll need to bypass the main thoroughfares," Kiero suggested, tracing a route on a holographic map projected from his wristband. "The Initiative's patrols are less frequent in the residential areas."

"That might work," another rebel chimed in, their eyes glinting with determination. "But we'll need to move quickly. The longer we're out in the open, the greater the risk of detection."

With a plan in place, they set out into the night, their senses heightened, alert to every sound and shadow. As they moved through the city streets, their hearts pounded with a mix of fear and determination, knowing that the Smile Enforcement Unit could be lurking around any corner.

"We're almost there," Heran whispered, a note of reassurance in his voice as they approached the outskirts of the city.

Suddenly, a voice crackled over a nearby speaker, echoing through the empty streets. "Attention all citizens. A curfew is now in effect. Please return to your homes immediately."

Heran, Kiero, and their fellow rebels quickened their pace, their eyes fixed on the horizon. Ahead, the city's towering walls loomed, separating them from the freedom they so desperately sought.

Approaching the city's edge, the faint hum of drones patrolling the skies above grew louder, ever-watchful eyes of the Smile Enforcement officers. Suddenly, without warning, a squad of officers descended upon them, their rifles blazing.

"Take cover!" Heran shouted, her voice barely audible over the deafening gunfire. Bullets whizzed past them, and screams of agony filled the air as several rebels fell, their bodies limp and lifeless.

Heran felt a surge of anger and grief at the loss of her fellow rebels, but she knew they couldn't afford to stop. "Keep moving! We can't let them win!" she yelled, her words a rallying cry for those still standing.

With Kiero at her side, Heran led the remaining rebels through the chaotic streets, dodging gunfire and weaving between abandoned buildings. The drones above buzzed overhead, their cameras scanning for any sign of movement.

"We need to find a way out," Kiero said. "We are close to the border of the Unity Party's territory. If we can make it there, we might have a chance."

They pressed on, their hearts pounding with fear and adrenaline. The journey was perilous, every step fraught with danger. But Heran and Kiero refused to give up. They fought with all their strength, using whatever weapons they could find to defend themselves. Kiero wielded a makeshift rifle, firing back at the officers with deadly accuracy, while Heran used her agility to evade their bullets, leading the group through alleyways and side streets.

"We're almost there," Heran said. "Just a little further."

After hours of grueling trekking through rugged terrain, Heran, Kiero, and the remaining rebels finally arrived at the border of the Unity Party's domain. Their bodies were weary, but their spirits were high, fueled by the hope of freedom that lay just beyond the towering wall that loomed before them.

When they approached the wall, they could hear the distant hum of drones patrolling the area. The rebels knew they had to proceed with caution. Suddenly, one of the drones spotted them and opened fire, its bullets whizzing dangerously close.

"Take cover!" Heran shouted, her voice echoing through the barren landscape. Reacting swiftly, Kiero took aim with his weapon and expertly shot down the drone, causing it to crash to the ground in a smoldering heap.

Heran gave signals to other rebels to be alert. "We need to keep moving. There may be more drones nearby."

The rebel pressed on, their hearts pounding with adrenaline as they approached the towering wall. The wall was guarded by armed soldiers and watchtowers equipped with powerful spotlights that illuminated the darkness.

"We need to find a way to breach that wall," Kiero announced in whisper tone. "Our freedom depends on it."

Heran nodded in agreement. "We'll need to create a diversion to distract the guards," she replied. "I have an idea."

With their comrades by their side, they formulated a daring plan. As the first light of dawn painted the sky in hues of orange and pink, casting long shadows over the desolate landscape, they launched their assault.

"Fire the smoke grenades!" Kiero shouted, his voice barely audibles over the chaos. Smoke filled the air, obscuring visibility, while the rebels opened fire, creating chaos and drawing the attention of the guards away from their intended point of entry.

Heran and Kiero led the rebels to the base of the wall. Ropes and grappling hooks were swiftly deployed, and with expert precision, they began their ascent. Each foothold and handhold were a calculated risk, the adrenaline-fueled climb a testament to their determination to escape the oppressive regime.

They finally reached the top, each catching their breath before descending the other side. The ground below offered a stark contrast to the fortified wall, a barren expanse stretching towards the horizon, devoid of life but brimming with possibility.

However, the cost of their escape was evident. Several of their comrades had fallen during the assault, their lifeless bodies a somber reminder of the sacrifices made for freedom.

"We'll never forget their sacrifice," Kiero sighed. "But their sacrifice will not be in vain. We will honor them by continuing the fight."

As they regrouped on the other side of the wall, Heran, Kiero, and the rebels felt a surge of relief and hope. The journey to freedom had been arduous, every step a calculated risk in their escape from the totalitarian grip of the Unity Party. Each member of the group bore the physical and emotional scars of their defiance, a testament to their unwavering determination to break free from oppression.

They moved with a cautious yet purposeful stride, their footsteps echoing in the stillness of the night. Heran, with her mechanical precision, led the way, her movements calculated and deliberate. Kiero, his eyes sharp and vigilant, scanned their surroundings, ever watchful for any signs of pursuit. The rebels followed closely behind, their faces set in grim determination, their resolve unshakable despite the dangers that lay ahead.

Their path took them through rugged terrain, the ground uneven beneath their feet. They navigated treacherous cliffs and steep inclines, their progress slow but steady. The barren wastelands they crossed seemed endless, the desolation mirroring the bleakness of their past lives under the Unity Party's rule.

Pressing on, they entered dense forests, the trees looming overhead like silent sentinels. The air was thick with the scent of pine and earth, the undergrowth rustling with unseen movement. They moved with caution, wary of any potential threats lurking in the shadows.

Finally, after days of hard travel, they reached the resistance camp, hidden deep in the mountains. The camp was a hive of activity, with rebels training for combat and preparing for the next phase of their fight against the Unity Party. As they entered the camp, a sense of solidarity washed over them, fueling their determination to see their mission through to the end.

But their joy at reaching the camp was short-lived, as they learned that the Unity Party had discovered their location and was preparing to launch a full-scale attack. The camp leaders knew that they had to act quickly if they were to have any chance of defending against the onslaught.

The sun began to set, its crimson glow casting an eerie light over the camp. Heran and Kiero joined the other rebels in preparing for battle, gathering around a makeshift map drawn in the dirt. They discussed their strategy, assigning each rebel a specific role: defending the perimeter, manning the watchtowers, or providing medical aid to the wounded.

Heran, with her expertise in mechanics, worked tirelessly to repair and fortify the camp's defenses. She reinforced the barricades, ensuring that they would withstand the impact of any enemy assault. Kiero, known for his sharpshooting skills, carefully cleaned and loaded his rifle, preparing for the moment when his accuracy would be needed most.

The tension hung I the air as the night wore on. The rebels knew that the coming battle would be the most challenging, but they were determined to stand their ground against the tyranny of the Unity Party. They took turns keeping watch, their eyes scanning the darkness for any sign of movement.

Finally, as the first light of dawn began to break on the horizon, the sound of approaching footsteps echoed through the camp. The Unity Party had arrived, their forces ready to crush the rebellion once and for all. But the rebels were prepared, their spirits unbroken, ready to fight for their freedom no matter the cost.

The attack came just before dawn, the Unity Party's forces descending upon the camp with a ferocity that shattered the pre-dawn silence. Gunfire erupted, the sharp cracks of rifles mixing with the deafening explosions of grenades and the screams of the wounded. Tracers streaked through the darkness, illuminating the chaos in flickering orange light.

Heran and Kiero fought side by side, their weapons blazing as they mowed down enemy soldiers with deadly accuracy. Heran's mechanical arm moved with mechanical precision, never wavering as she targeted enemy combatants with lethal efficiency. Kiero's shots were equally deadly, each bullet finding its mark with deadly accuracy.

The air was thick with the acrid smell of gunpowder and the metallic tang of blood as the two sides clashed in a brutal, bloody battle. Bullets flew past them, whizzing dangerously close as they sought cover behind overturned tables and sandbags. Heran felt a searing pain in her shoulder as a bullet grazed her, but she gritted her teeth and fought on, fueled by a fierce determination to protect her comrades.

Kiero's movements were swift and fluid, his combat training evident as he ducked and weaved through the chaos. He moved with purpose, his eyes scanning the battlefield for targets as he returned fire with lethal precision. He seemed almost like a ghost, appearing and disappearing amidst the smoke and gunfire.

But the Unity Party's forces were relentless, their numbers overwhelming the rebels at every turn. Heran and Kiero found themselves surrounded, their backs against the wall as the enemy closed in. Despite their best efforts, the tide of battle began to turn against them.

In a last desperate bid for survival, Heran threw herself at the enemy, using her body as a shield to protect Kiero from the hail of bullets. She felt the impact of the enemy's weapons against her flesh, but she refused to yield, fighting with a courage born of desperation.

As the enemy soldiers closed in, their weapons raised for the final blow, a voice rang out from the darkness, stopping them in their tracks. It was the leader of the resistance, standing tall and defiant, his weapon raised high.

"Stop!" he shouted. "These are not your enemies. They are our comrades, fighting for freedom against tyranny."

The enemy soldiers hesitated, unsure of what to do. The leader seized the opportunity, rallying the rebels and launching a counterattack that caught the Unity Party's forces off guard.

In the chaos that followed, Heran and Kiero fought their way to safety, their bodies battered and bruised but their spirits unbroken. They knew that the battle was far from over, but they also knew that as long as they stood together, they had a chance of overthrowing the Unity Party and bringing an end to their oppressive rule.

The sun rose over the mountains, casting a warm glow over the battlefield, as the rebels gathered to survey the aftermath of the battle. The Unity Party's forces lay scattered across the ground, their weapons abandoned as they fled or surrendered to the victorious rebels.

Heran and Kiero stood among her comrades, her heart heavy with the weight of what they had achieved. The camp was in ruins, but it was a small price to pay for the freedom they had won. The rebels set to work again rebuilding their camp and caring for the wounded. Days turned into weeks, and weeks turned into months as the rebels worked tirelessly to establish a new government. With Heran at the helm, they drafted a constitution that guaranteed freedom of speech, assembly, and expression. They abolished the Smile Detection Initiative and dismantled the oppressive surveillance state that had once ruled their lives.

But Heran and Kiero knew that true change would only come with the removal of the Unity Party's leaders, the ones who had orchestrated their oppression for so long. She knew that it was up to her to confront them, to hold them accountable for their crimes against humanity.

With a small group of trusted rebels at her side, Kiero and Heran went on the perilous journey to find and confront the leaders of the Unity Party. They tracked the elusive figures to a remote compound nestled deep in the unforgiving mountains, where they had sought refuge after their defeat.

The rebels approached the compound under the cloak of darkness. The night was thick with tension, and as they neared the compound, the rebels moved with the precision of shadows, avoiding the remaining sentries and slipping through the cracks in the enemy's defenses.

Inside the compound, the rebels encountered minimal resistance, the guards having been decimated in the earlier conflict. Their path to the inner sanctum was eerily quiet, the only sounds the soft footfalls of their party and the distant hum of machinery.

Finally, they reached the heart of the compound, where the leaders of the Unity Party had barricaded themselves. Kiero's voice cut through the silence, demanding their surrender and accountability for their crimes. But the leaders, desperate and cornered, refused to yield. With a defiant roar, they raised their weapons, signaling the beginning of a brutal and bloody showdown.

The battle unfolded in a whirlwind of chaos and violence, gunfire reverberating off the walls as bodies dropped and blood spilled. The rebels fought with a ferocity fueled by righteous fury, Heran and Kiero moving with a deadly grace and unwavering determination.

Bullets whizzed past Heran, the air thick with the acrid stench of gunpowder and the anguished cries of the wounded. Her comrades fought beside her, their determination unyielding as they advanced, steadily closing the gap to their targets.

As Heran closed in on the leaders of the Unity Party, her heart hammered in her chest, adrenaline surging through her veins. She could see the fear in their eyes, a stark contrast to the arrogance that once defined them. They knew their time had come, justice finally catching up with them.

In a last desperate attempt to save themselves, the leaders of the Unity Party raised their weapons, but it was too late. The rebels were faster, their aim true as they unleashed a torrent of bullets that cut the tyrants down where they stood.

The first leader, once ensnared by the allure of dominance, staggered backward with a stricken expression as a bullet tore through his chest. His eyes widened in disbelief, grappling with the sudden onslaught, before his strength waned, and he collapsed to the ground, the weight of his power extinguished in an instant.

The second leader, a woman known for her cruelty and ambition, tried to flee, but she couldn't evade the rebels' gunfire. A bullet struck her leg, causing her to collapse. She cried out in pain, but before she could crawl to safety, another shot silenced her for good.

As the dust settled and the smoke cleared, Heran stood victorious, her enemies defeated at her feet. She had succeeded in removing the last vestiges of the Unity Party's tyranny, paving the way for a new era of peace and prosperity.

Looking out at the world before her, Heran knew that the road ahead would be long and arduous. But she also knew that she had overcome the greatest obstacle of all: fear. Then, something unexpected happened. Heran's comrades, those hardened rebels who had fought alongside her, began to laugh. It was a joyous, infectious sound, filling the air with a sense of relief and freedom.

Heran joined in, her laughter mingling with theirs. And as she laughed, she felt something strange and wonderful happen. She felt a smile spread across her face, a genuine, unbridled smile that reached her eyes for the first time in as long as she could remember. Kiero ran to her and claimed her kiss. Their kiss was intimate and after the kiss, Heran and Kiero genuinely smiles.

About the Author

BlackMiere

BlackMiere, a registered author at the National Book Development Board Philippines, a wattpad, and published author. With a knack for imaginative storytelling, he ventures into various genres. A fervent enthusiast of mystery-thriller films, he's often captivated by late-night horror movies, particularly possession and exorcism movies. While his primary focus is on BL writing, BlackMiere eagerly embraces the opportunity to explore new genres, including thriller and science fiction, as he continues to expand his creative horizons.

www.ingramcontent.com/pod-product-compliance
Lightning Source LLC
LaVergne TN
LVHW041633070526
838199LV00052B/3343